The Usborne
Big Book
of Bugs

Written by Emily Bone

Illustrated by Fabiano Fiorin

Designed by Stephen Wright

Bugs expert: Dr. Naomi Ewald

Usborne Quicklinks

For links to websites where you can find out more about bugs, go to the Usborne Quicklinks website at **www.usborne.com/quicklinks** and type in the title of this book. Please follow the internet safety guidelines at the Usborne Quicklinks website.

How big is BIG?

There are millions of different bugs. Lots of them are very small but others are HUGE. The bugs in this book are shown about the same size as they are in real life.

Some big bugs use their bodies to scare away attackers. The **giant jungle nymph** stands up on its front legs and thrashes its body around.

The **giant huntsman spider** is the BIGGEST SPIDER in the world.

It lays some of the largest eggs of any insect.

The **Saint Helena giant earwig** is about eight times bigger than a **common earwig.**

Common earwig

Some flying bugs have very big wings.

The **blue morpho butterfly** is one of the biggest butterflies.

The **rhinoceros beetle** is very strong. It can carry 800 times its own weight – the same as a person carrying 4 elephants.

The **pygmy blue butterfly** is the world's smallest butterfly.

The **regal moth** is one of the biggest moths – but it lives for just one week.

Wonderful wings

Flying bugs have thin wings that they flap very quickly to stay up in the air. They use them to reach food and fly away from danger.

Giant mydas flies look like giant wasps, so other bugs don't eat them.

Moths use their feathery antennae (feelers) to find partners.

The **atlas moth** is the BIGGEST FLYING BUG in the world.

`Hercules caterpillars` are covered in poisonous spikes.

When a **giant bush cricket** flies, its wings look like big leaves. This hides it from potential attackers.

West African antlions have long, speckled wings. This makes it difficult for attackers to spot them in the dry, brown grassland where they live.

The **white witch moth** has the LONGEST WINGS of any bug. When fully open, they would stretch from the top to the bottom of this page.

Queen Alexandra's caterpillars have bright red and yellow markings. This warns other creatures that they're poisonous.

Giant dobsonflies have a wingspan of over 20cm (8in).

The bigger a giant dobsonfly's jaws, the more likely he is to attract a female.

Lots of legs

All bugs have at least six legs, but some have lots more. They help them to run fast, climb and hunt for food.

The **rhinoceros cockroach** has spiky legs to dig burrows into hard ground.

The **imperial moth caterpillar** is the LARGEST CATERPILLAR in the world.

While it's hiding in the undergrowth, a **Mexican redknee tarantula** can sense whether there is another spider, or something good to eat, walking past.

The caterpillar uses its legs to climb up tree branches so it can eat the leaves. After a month, it will turn into a moth.

An **emperor scorpion** uses its big claws to grab and crush prey.

A **camel spider** senses food through hairs on its front legs.

It carries its babies to keep them safe.

These aren't actually legs. They're feelers used to sense food.

It eats small lizards and mice. Its long legs help it to chase down prey.

It uses its big jaws to dig burrows where it can hide from the hot sun.

When a birdeater is frightened, it shakes poisonous hairs off its back.

It kills big bugs, mice and lizards with its big fangs. But it hardly ever eats birds.

Hidden bugs

Some bugs look like other things,
which makes them difficult to spot.
This hides them from attackers,
and also helps them to catch prey.

Groups of **thorn bugs** cling
to branches. Their spiky green bodies
are similar to thorns on a stem.

A **Chan's megastick**
can be as long as an
adult's arm. It stays
hidden in trees
as it looks like
a twig.

Bird dropping spiders' bodies are
covered in white silk. Other creatures
think the spiders are droppings,
so they don't get eaten.

It's hard to
see this
**giant leaf
insect** on
a leafy
green plant.

They also hide
under leaves.

Leaf insects'
bodies, legs and
heads look
like leaves.

The **dead leaf
butterfly's** wings
are brown and
crinkled, like
dead leaves.

Lots of legs

All bugs have at least six legs, but some have lots more. They help them to run fast, climb and hunt for food.

The **rhinoceros cockroach** has spiky legs to dig burrows into hard ground.

While it's hiding in the undergrowth, a **Mexican redknee tarantula** can sense whether there is another spider, or something good to eat, walking past.

An **emperor scorpion** uses its big claws to grab and crush prey.

It carries its babies to keep them safe.

These aren't actually legs. They're feelers used to sense food.

Hercules caterpillars are covered in poisonous spikes.

When a **giant bush cricket** flies, its wings look like big leaves. This hides it from potential attackers.

West African antlions have long, speckled wings. This makes it difficult for attackers to spot them in the dry, brown grassland where they live.

The **white witch moth** has the LONGEST WINGS of any bug. When fully open, they would stretch from the top to the bottom of this page.

The bigger a giant dobsonfly's jaws, the more likely he is to attract a female.

The **imperial moth caterpillar** is the LARGEST CATERPILLAR in the world.

The caterpillar uses its legs to climb up tree branches so it can eat the leaves. After a month, it will turn into a moth.

A **camel spider** senses food through hairs on its front legs.

It eats small lizards and mice. Its long legs help it to chase down prey.

It uses its big jaws to dig burrows where it can hide from the hot sun.

Queen Alexandra's caterpillars have bright red and yellow markings. This warns other creatures that they're poisonous.

Giant dobsonflies have a wingspan of over 20cm (8in).

Golden silk orb-weaving spiders weave huge webs that can be as tall as a two-floor house.

Peruvian yellowleg centipedes can have around 40 legs. Their front legs are filled with poison to kill prey.

A **giant African black millipede** has up to 250 legs – the most of any bug.

The **goliath birdeater spider** is one of the largest spiders in the world.

Giant helicopter damselflies have long wings that look like a helicopter's rotor.

A **giant hawker dragonfly** can fly up to 40km/h (25mph). That's as fast as a sprinter.

Hercules moths are also called swallowtail moths, because the bottoms of their wings look like birds' tails.

The **Queen Alexandra's birdwing butterfly** is the world's BIGGEST BUTTERFLY.

Deadliest bugs

Armed with sharp jaws, painful stings or deadly poison, some bugs are very harmful to other bugs, animals or humans.

In real life, the tsetse fly is only this big.

It's shown bigger here so you can see it more clearly.

Tsetse fly
Female tsetse flies bite people and animals to suck out the blood. They pass on deadly diseases.

The non-flying dorylus is actually very small. It's shown bigger here so you can see what it looks like.

Black widow spider
Black widows bite their prey and inject a deadly poison at the same time.

Non-flying dorylus actual size

Flying dorylus

Saddleback caterpillar
Saddleback caterpillars' bright green and red markings warn other animals not to eat them.

Dorylus ant
Dorylus ants devour any creature that gets in their way.

Lonomia caterpillar
Lonomia caterpillars are covered in extremely poisonous hairs.

The fattail scorpion's sting is in the end of its tail.

Giant water bug
Water bugs live underwater. They have sharp mouthparts that they use to stab prey.

Fattail scorpion
The fattail scorpion is the world's MOST DANGEROUS SCORPION. The poison in its sting can kill a person.

Assassin bugs hunt other bugs. An assassin will stab a bug with its sharp mouth parts, then suck out the insides.

If they're attacked, they spit a poisonous liquid in their attacker's eyes.

Giant water bugs eat bugs and small animals, including frogs and turtles. They grab prey with their strong front legs, then inject them with poison.

A **giant vinegaroon** seizes beetles or spiders, then uses its fearsome jaws to crush them.

The **Brazilian wandering spider** is the MOST POISONOUS BUG in the world. It lurks in the undergrowth, then quickly bites passing bugs to kill them for food.

Giant Asian hornets chase after prey, then use their poisonous sting to kill.

You'll know when it's about to attack because its face goes bright red.

Giant hornets can fly very fast, so they don't let tasty bugs, like this cicada, get away.

Saddleback caterpillars have very poisonous bodies. Any creature that eats them will become very sick, or even die.

If you brush against a **lonomia caterpillar**, its hairs will make your skin swell up and become very painful.

Hummingbird hawk moths look like small birds called hummingbirds. This stops birds from eating them.

Young thorn bugs are called nymphs. Their bodies have the same pattern as bark on a tree.

Orchid mantises stay hidden in flowers. They eat small insects that land on the flower.

The **giant Asian mantis** hides in green plants.

The other sides of its wings are patterned.

Assassin bug
Assassin bugs hide under dead leaves, then jump out and attack their prey.

Giant Asian hornet
Giant hornets attack big bugs and nests of bees. A hornet can kill 40 bees in a minute.

Bullet ant
Of all insects, bullet ants have the MOST PAINFUL STING. They will attack intruders to their nests.

The acid is like vinegar, which is how the vinegaroon got its name.

Fangs

Giant vinegaroon
If a giant vinegaroon is attacked, it will spray stinging acid from its tail.

Sydney funnel spider
The Sydney funnel spider has big fangs to inject poison into its prey.

Giant tarantula hawk wasp
Giant hawk wasps hunt some of the biggest spiders in the world, including the goliath birdeater spider.

Brazilian wandering spider
Brazilian wandering spiders hide in plants, then jump out and bite their prey.

Black widow spiders catch bugs in big webs.

You can spot a black widow by the red markings on the underside of its body.

A **fattail scorpion** hides in dark corners, then stings crickets as they pass by. Poison from the sting dissolves the cricket's insides.

Dorylus ants have very strong mouthparts.

The scorpion uses these pincers to pin down prey before stinging it.

Bullet ants sting if they're attacked. The sting is extremely painful, and lasts for a whole day. They also have a nasty bite.

Dorylus ants move around in big groups, to find a place to nest. They can eat a whole rat in minutes.

Flying dorylus are nicknamed sausage flies because they have sausage-shaped bodies.

Giant tarantula hawk wasps kill spiders with a powerful sting. Female wasps drag the spiders back to their nests, then use them as food for young wasps.

Big beetles

Beetles are some of the biggest and heaviest bugs. They eat natural waste, including rotting wood and fruit, and even dung.

Goliath beetles use their spiky legs to cling onto trees so they can eat fruit and bark.

Actaeon beetles are the HEAVIEST BUGS in the world. They weigh as much as a grapefruit.

Elephant beetles have long horns for fighting other beetles.

Hercules beetles can push up to 850 times their own weight – the same as a person pushing 10 large cars.

The **titan beetle** has the BIGGEST BODY of any bug. It's as large as a rat and its jaws are so strong, they can bite through a pencil.

A **giraffe stag beetle's** jaws look like antlers. It uses them to fight other beetles. The winner is the first to push his enemy off the branch.

A **sawyer beetle's** huge jaws frighten away other bugs. But they aren't very powerful and wouldn't actually hurt you.

Monarch butterflies fly for weeks every winter to escape the harsh cold. They land on trees to rest every few days.

When they're together, the butterflies' bright, patterned wings confuse attackers.

Termite nests are home to thousands of termites. Workers patrol the nest, repairing any damage.

Every year **honey bees** look for a new place to build a nest. They gather in big swarms, like this, before they set off.

A swarm of **locusts** devours an enormous amount of food per day – as much as 450 million people would eat in the same period.

Gigantic groups

Some bugs live together in huge groups, or form big swarms. Some of these bugs are very small, so they're shown larger here than they really are.

Desert locust
Group size: up to 40 billion
After it rains, locusts form massive swarms to feed and find mates.

The bugs' actual sizes are shown here.

The queen termite has a big, white body.

Fire ant
Group size: up to 500,000
Fire ants live in huge nests. The queen lays 1,000 eggs per day.

Mound building termite
Group size: over 1 million
Termites build very tall nests – over 9m (30ft) high.

They collect pollen from flowers in tiny pouches on their legs.

Honey bee
Group size: up to 10,000
Bees make honey from pollen, and use it to feed their young.

Actual sizes

Yellowjacket wasp
Group size: 5,000
Yellowjackets make nests from chewed-up wood.

Actual size

Monarch butterfly
Group size: over 100 million
Monarch butterflies fly from North America to Mexico every winter.

Mosquito
Group size: over a million
Swarms of mosquitos fly over rivers and lakes. Females have a nasty bite.

Actual size

Actual size

Actual size

Actual size

Colorado potato beetle
Group size: up to 30,000
Colorado beetles can devour whole potato or tomato crops.

House fly
Group size: up to 1,000
Big swarms of house flies feed on rotting waste.

Asian lady beetle
Group size: thousands
Asian lady beetles flock to warm, sunny surfaces.

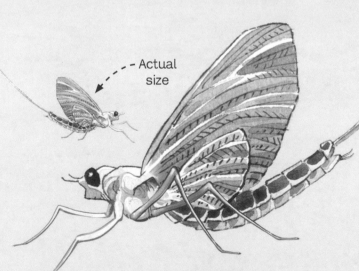

Lake flies are very small. A swarm looks like this.

Male lake flies use their feathery antennae (feelers) to find females.

Empress cicada
Group size: Hundreds of millions
Cicadas swarm to find a mate. Males create a very loud 'song' – as loud as a jumbo jet's engine – to attract females.

Lake fly
Group size: many millions
Lake fly swarms are so big they look like thick, black clouds.

Actual size

Mayfly
Group size: thousands
Mayfly young live underwater. They come to the surface to turn into adults and find mates.

Purple crow butterfly
Group size: over 11,000
Purple crow butterflies gather in massive groups to find warmer weather in the winter.

Termites spend most of their time in underground chambers, caring for the queen. She lays over 30,000 eggs a day.

Asian lady beetles need to stay warm in order to survive. When it gets colder, they swarm in warm, sunny places.

As soon as anything touches the top of a fire ant's nest, the ants rush out to sting the intruder.

Adult **mayflies** only live for a few hours. In this time, they find a mate and lay hundreds of eggs.

A section of the termite mound has been cut away. These tunnels allow air to flow, keeping the nest cool.

Strongest, heaviest, longest...

Here are some more fascinating bugs, both big and small...

Horseflies fly FASTER than any other bug. They can reach 144km/h (90mph) – the speed of a fast car.

Jewel beetles are the world's LONGEST-LIVED BUG. The oldest jewel beetle lived for 47 years.

Jewel beetles' bodies are covered in tiny scales that sparkle in the sunlight.

The **mole cricket** uses its shovel-like feet to dig long 6m (20ft) burrows.

The **dung beetle** is the STRONGEST BUG. It can push up to 1,141 times its own weight – like a person lifting six double-decker buses.

The **Madagascan hawk moth** feeds on a flower called the comet orchid.

It sucks nectar from the orchid's nectar tube with its 28cm (11in) long tongue.

Dung beetles roll balls of dung for their young to eat.

Comet orchid's nectar tube: moths push their tongues into this tube to suck out the nectar.

The **giant wood moth** is the HEAVIEST MOTH in the world. It weighs as much as a small orange.

The **stink bug** is the SMELLIEST BUG of all. It releases a very smelly liquid when it's frightened.

Antennae

Asian longhorn beetles have very long antennae (feelers). They are longer than the beetle's whole body.

Series designer: Laura Wood   Series editor: Jane Chisholm
Additional design: Emily Barden and Helen Edmonds   Image manipulation: John Russell